For Tim and Kate's baby.

Published by Delacorte Press
Bantam Doubleday Dell Publishing Group, Inc.
666 Fifth Avenue, New York, New York 10103

This edition was first published in Great Britain in 1989 by Walker Books Ltd., London.

The trademark Delacorte Press® is registered in the U.S. Patent and Trademark Office.

Library of Congress Cataloging-in-Publication Data
Riddell, Chris.
When the walrus comes / Chris Riddell.
p.   cm.
Summary: A boy and his walrus friend sail to an island crowded with monkeys, where
they teach each other their favorite activities and have a great time playing.
ISBN 0-385-29858-7
[1. Walruses — Fiction. 2. Monkeys — Fiction.] I. Title.
PZ7.R41618Wh   1990   89-31718
[E] — dc19   CIP
                                                                          AC

Manufactured in Italy
First U.S.A. printing March 1990
10 9 8 7 6 5 4 3 2 1

WHEN THE
WALRUS COMES

Written and Illustrated by

Chris Riddell

Delacorte
Press

It's always fun when
the walrus comes to visit.

It's fun when we do things

and fun when we don't.

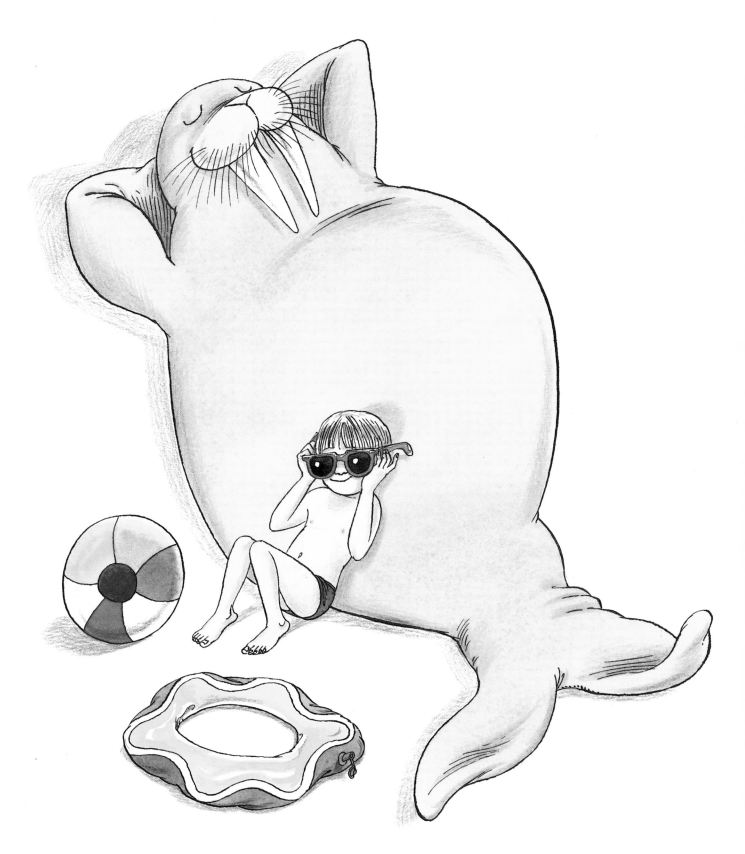

One day we packed our bags

and set sail in the *Phoebe McBean*.

We sailed up

and down

and around and around

until . . .

we came to an island where monkeys live.

The monkeys helped us unpack,

and they helped us eat our sandwiches.

They showed us all the things monkeys like to do, like climbing trees,

and swinging on vines

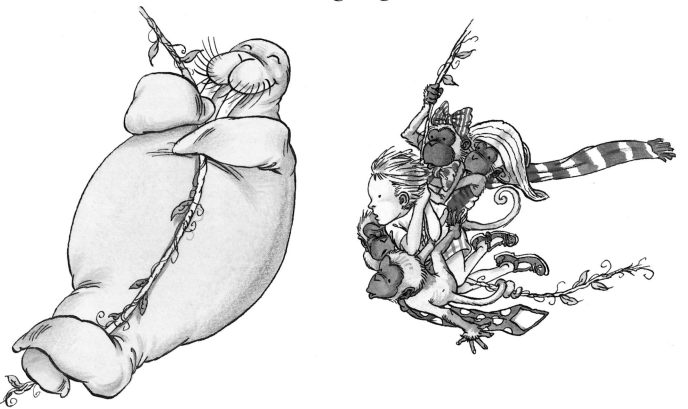

and hanging upside down.

And we showed them what we like to do,

like standing on our heads

and doing cartwheels

and making silly faces.

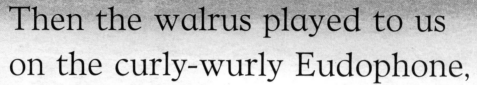

Then the walrus played to us
on the curly-wurly Eudophone,

and we had fun being noisy.

And we had fun being quiet
when the moon and stars came out.

That's how it is–

it's always fun

when the walrus comes to visit.